The Weaver's Son
&
other stories

Copyright © Subrata Roy 2019

All rights reserved. No part of this publication may be reproduced, distributed, or transmitted in any form or by any means, including photocopying, recording, or other electronic or mechanical methods, without the prior written permission of the publisher, except in the case of brief quotations embodied in critical reviews and certain other non-commercial uses permitted by copyright law.

This is a work of fiction. Names, characters, places and incidents are either the product of the author's imagination or are used fictitiously, and any resemblance to actual persons, living or dead, events or locales is entirely coincidental.

In loving memory of Bapi, my father.

Table of Contents

The Weaver's Son…………………………………………9

The Neighbour……………………………………14

Piku & Chiki……………………………………...21

The Clock……………………………………...26

Bravery…………………………………………32

Dolphins…………………………………………….38

The Letter……………………………………………...42

For Humanity's Sake…………………………………48

White Lilies……………………………………………52

Foreword & Acknowledgements

I was initiated into the world of books by my father. Every Wednesday, we would head over to the British Library in my hometown Ranchi, in India. I loved the smell of books and have very fond memories of the library. In those days, we didn't even have a landline in our home, let alone mobile phones or internet. The library was my connection to the external world, apart from the daily newspaper. I remember watching the marriage of Prince Charles and Princess Diana, which was screened specially for the patrons of the library. Little did I know, that twenty years from then, I would be walking the very streets of London through which their carriage travelled.

As it invariably happens in India, reading books took a back seat once the pressure of public exams took their hold on my life. I never got back to reading in the same way as I did when I was a child. But I loved to think. There would be brief flashes of ideas that came to me from time to time. I would try to develop these in my head but was too busy to flesh them out. I finally got an opportunity this year to nurture and give shape to my thoughts. While the ideas were in the realm of fiction, as I started to write, I felt like expressing my experiences and learnings in my life, wrapped around those fictional ideas. These have taken the shape of nine short stories, which I present before you.

Having lived in multiple geographies (India, United Kingdom and France) and travelled around the globe, I have been fortunate to observe and experience how people live and interact in different parts of the world. While this has influenced the choice of settings and context behind my stories, the lens through which I have interpreted these events has been largely shaped by my own experiences during my childhood. I can't say if it is true for everyone, but the more life has changed for me, the more it has remained the same.

I do hope you will enjoy reading the stories.

I would like to thank a number of people for their encouragement and feedback in this journey.

My wife (Madhu) and my twin sons (Sukant & Sumant) for being my strongest supporters and worst critics.

My mother for giving me the childhood that has helped shape my understanding of life.

My friends from my alma mater IIT Roorkee, who encouraged me to write, despite the crazy plots I shared with them

Last but not the least, Divya Jha, who provided such wonderful feedback on the stories.

The Weaver's Son

I was about to turn off the bed lamp when the phone rang. It was eleven in the night by the bedside clock. Stretching out over my wife Anita, who was fast asleep beside me, I lifted the receiver. A familiar voice greeted me on the other side. "Sir, I am sorry to disturb you, but you need to come urgently. There has been a murder." I noted down the address and told Amit I would be there in fifteen minutes.

I tiptoed out of our room, careful not to wake up Anita and changed into my uniform. Leaving a note for her on the dining table, I drove off in the darkness. As I approached the scene of crime, I could see Amit at the entrance of the house instructing the other policemen. He saluted me as I approached. "Give me the brief," I said walking into the house.

It was a sparse room. A large sofa sat in one corner, its uneven bulges indicating years of use. A small coffee table with an ornate top stood in front of it. Behind the sofa was a huge portrait. "This is Mushtaq's father," explained Amit. "He was a weaver and Mushtaq inherited this business from his father. He was probably the best weaver in this town, has a workshop near the local market."

There were signs of a struggle. A couple of reclining chairs lay upturned on the floor. A large vase next to the chairs had broken into pieces. The carpet was in disarray. Mushtaq himself, was sprawled on the ground, face down. The photographers and fingerprint specialists were kneeling beside him, carefully collecting evidence.

"There must have been at least two people to subdue a well-built person like Mushtaq," muttered Amit. I nodded, my gaze shifting to a photograph on the mantelpiece. Amit followed my gaze and said, "That is his son, Salim. He is in the other room." He turned his head to where the curtains were. "He was here when this happened, but he doesn't know a thing. He was in his room and did not hear anything. The poor child is deaf and dumb," he added.

"I would like to see him," I said walking towards the curtains. As I went inside, I saw a small boy perched up on his bed. "He must be about four feet tall," I thought, judging by how far his legs dangled over the floor. He was wearing a light blue T shirt and dark blue shorts. "Hello, I am Inspector Rupak," I said extending my hand. The boy did not respond. I sat next to him. He looked at me, his eyes betrayed fear. "Did you see anything," I asked. He seemed not to hear me. I remembered what Amit had said. I patted his shoulder

10

and got up to go. "Amit!" I called out. "Does he have any relatives." "Oh Yes Sir, he has an aunt who lives a few kilometres away. She is on her way and will be here any moment," Amit shouted back.

There was nothing more to do here, so I asked Amit to oversee things and report to me in the morning. As I drove back, I thought of Mushtaq's son and felt sorry for him.

Weeks passed by and we made very little progress in the case. Salim's aunt was of no help. She hardly knew his friends or acquaintances. The neighbours had not heard anything. As for Salim, he had gone into a shell, afraid to meet anybody. I asked Amit to leave him in peace. "Good that his aunt is there to look after him," I thought.

Anita's birthday was approaching and as usual I was having a hard time deciding on a suitable gift. "Why don't I gift her something from the weaver's shop?" I thought. "It will be a nice gesture to buy something from them – it must be hard for the boy. I will give him some extra money." Feeling happy with my decision, I went off to the market. After some enquiries, I managed to find the shop. There was an old man at the counter who introduced himself as Mushtaq' uncle. "I am running the shop now," he explained. I told him I wanted to buy a shawl and asked if there were any I could see now. "We don't stock shawls Sir," he said. "You will need to order one and we will weave it for you." I was about to order one when I checked myself. "Who weaves nowadays, now that Mushtaq is no more." "That is no problem sir,

Mushtaq's son Salim is a skilled weaver. He is young but has the magic in his fingers that his father had. Of course, he will take a week more, but you will not regret buying it." Eager to help the family as much as I could, I ordered the most expensive shawl. "It would be delivered in two weeks Sir," the old man said. "Yes, yes I know where you live," he assured me.

Two weeks later, as I was about to go out to the club, there was a knock on the door. I opened the door to see Salim. He had the same blue T shirt but looked visibly thinner than what I had seen him that night. There was a brown packet in his hand. "It must be the shawl," I thought, taking it from his outstretched hands. I reached for my wallet, but he shook his head, turned his back and walked out through the gate. I called out ..but he didn't look back. "I'll go to his shop and give the money to the old man," I thought, closing the door. The shawl had come on time, as next day was my wife's birthday.

"Why don't we try the new Italian restaurant for your birthday," I suggested, as I got into my car in the morning. Later that evening, I gave her the shawl. "It is beautiful, exactly the colour I wanted" she said hugging me. We went out for dinner after a couple of hours. It was spring but she took the shawl for the night. Once in the restaurant, Anita went to the restroom. As I waited for her, I reached out for the shawl she had left on her chair. "I haven't even seen it properly," I mused. I felt the soft luxurious silk and held it up against the light. The embroidery was indeed intricate and glistened in the light. Something caught my eye and I froze.

The events of the fateful night unfolded in my hands, exquisitely woven into the shawl. There were three men, holding down Mushtaq. One man in a pink floral shirt was strangling Mushtaq with a blue scarf.... I could see a boy peeping through a hole in the door....

"Are you alright? You look shaken," said Anita, interrupting my thoughts. "Oh, Yes I am," I stammered. "I was just admiring the shawl," I said, handing it back to her.

The next day, we caught the culprits. I remembered that I owed money for the shawl, so made my way to Mushtaq's shop. His uncle was there and as soon as I entered, he reached out and hugged me. He had heard the news of the arrests. I gave him the money and asked, "Where is Salim? "He is in the workshop," he said looking back over his shoulder.

I stepped through the door into the workshop and found Salim crouched over the loom, busy at work. I went over to him and gently placed my hand on his shoulder. He looked up at me and instinctively reached out with his hand. I held him tightly as his eyes welled up in tears.

The Neighbour

Graham's van laboured up through the winding roads, the sunshine filtering through the windows. He squinted and reached out for his sunglasses in the glove box. He glanced at his watch - it was eleven thirty. "Half an hour more to go," he thought to himself. He turned around a sharp corner and hit the cobbled streets of Eze. It was a typical village in France, with its quaint boulangeries and cafes. Very soon he was at the door step of his new house. His house stood on a cliff, overlooking the sea. It was a quiet place, exactly what he needed to write his book.

As he unloaded his stuff on the patio, someone called out. He turned around and saw a woman in a pink dress at the gate.

"*Bonjour Monsieur!* I Madame Camille, your neighbour. I live here close and was walking when I see you. I want to meet you, I think to myself," she said visibly struggling with her English.

Graham took her outstretched hand, made a quick bow and introduced himself. After exchanging some pleasantries, Madame Camille excused herself. But she made sure that she had invited Graham to her house. "It just over the cliff, by the pine trees," she reminded him for the fifth time. Graham promised to visit her soon and turned his attention to the more important tasks in front of him.

After a few hours, he was tired. He must have dozed off, before he woke up to the sound of the doorbell. He opened the door to find Madame Camille at the door. "I am sorry, *Monsieur,*" she said. "I hope I not disturb you. I bring some croissants for you; the village shops close early, and I am not sure you had anything to eat at home." Graham, who was still groggy with sleep, stared at the croissants and then at Madame Camille. "Why don't you come in Madame?" he offered, opening the door wide. "*Merci beaucoup* for these croissants. I was going to make myself some tea, please do have some with me."

"*Non, non Monsieur*, I will go. My children at home and they are up to some mischief definitely. But you come over tomorrow evening," she said, waving from the gate.

It was almost noon when Graham woke up the next day. As he drew the blinds, the bright sun lit up the entire room. He could see the blue sea at short distance. The sky was clear with a few specks of white clouds. Some children were running down the streets. He could see two girls with pig tails, closely followed by Madame

15

Camille. These must be Madame's daughters, he thought. As he sat on the veranda overlooking the sea, Graham was already feeling happy with his decision to buy this place. It had not been easy though. The agent had kept him on the edge till the last moment. He had paid about five thousand euros more than his budget. But it was well worth it, he thought. I can live here in peace and focus on finishing my book.

It was almost evening when he remembered Madame Camille's invitation. "It is not too late," he thought. "I should pay a visit, otherwise it would seem rude." As it was a bit chilly outside, he got himself a light flannel jacket and headed out towards the pine trees.

The house was nestled close to the trees, barely visible from the road. He wouldn't have found it, hadn't Madame Camille given the instructions. He opened the wooden gate and stepped into the garden. There were flowers everywhere – roses, dahlias, chrysanthemums and lilies. A large pine tree stood at one side of the garden. There was a bench under the tree. The perfect spot to write a book, he mused, as he knocked on the front door. He waited for a few seconds. He could hear voices at a distance, children playing. He rapped the door a second time and could soon hear scurrying footsteps. Madame Camille opened the door. Her eyes lit up when she saw him. "*Bonjour Monsieur, bienvenue.* Please come in," she said, guiding him down a narrow passage to the living room.

The room was very tastefully decorated – two sets of floral sofas, a leather armchair with a heavily carved coffee table in between. The curtains were of silk with embroidery at the edges. A book case stood in one of the corners. A tall brass lamp lit up the room in soft white light. A large mirror hung over the fireplace. Very French, he thought.

"Sit down, *s'il vous plaît*, said Madame Camille, waving him towards one of the sofas. She sat opposite him, in the leather chair. She was wearing a printed blue skirt and a light grey top. She had brown eyes and golden hair up to her shoulders. "She must be about forty-five years old," he thought.

"What will you have Monsieur. Café or tea?" Graham gestured that he didn't want to have any, but she would have none of it. Finally, he settled for tea. "I come back in a few minutes, "she said. You pick up some book, maybe you find something interesting." She returned with the tea and tray full of homemade cookies. "They are delicious," said Graham, biting into the cookies. Just then, two girls rushed into the room.

"Be careful," said Madame Camille. "You disturb Monsieur. Now, go in garden and play. But come back soon and have the cakes in the kitchen." The girls rushed out, giggling.

"They are my daughters – Florence and Helene," explained Madame Camille. "They very naughty and run around the house all the time. My boy, Pascal, is much more well behaved. He like to have fun but in his own quiet way. He is inside his room, probably reading a book." "We have lived here for the last fifteen years, she went on. "My children are born here. My husband is in the navy, he spends six months at sea in the ships. He come back in August; you should meet him then. Florence and Helene are like their Dad – always laughing and up to some mischief. Pascal is different. He is more like my father, who was into books all the time." Her eyes moistened as she talked about him.

They chatted away late into the evening. It was getting dark, she opened the main door and called out to her daughters. Florence and Helene came in, out of breath with all the running around. "Go and wash yourself," Madame Carline told them. "There's cake in the kitchen. But remember to give Pascal some. He will otherwise forget to eat."

I remembered I had to get some milk for tomorrow and got up to go. "It is very kind of you for coming," said Madame Camille. "It is entirely my pleasure," Graham said, as he looked around for his flannel jacket. He finally spotted it on the hook next to the door. "*Bonne nuit*," she said, closing the door after him.

A week passed by and Graham had already fallen in love with this place. He would wake up to the cries of sea gulls in the morning. A leisurely breakfast of poached eggs and croissants would be followed by a walk through the village streets, breathing in the salty air of the sea. The weather had been good last week, with bright sunshine all day long. He was also making good progress on his book. Every day, he would see Madame Camille walking down the road with her daughters in tow. She would wave at him and sometimes he would go out and chat with them, standing at the gate. Her husband came over during the summer. He was tall and well-built and had a great sense of humour. He doted on his daughters and they would always by his side wherever he went. Graham would visit their house every weekend. Madame Camille was an excellent cook and she would insist that they have dinner together on those days. Graham protested initially but over the weeks, he had developed a close bond with her and the family. Dinner time was full of fun and laughter. The girls were beginning to learn English at school and tried to practice with Graham, getting it wrong half the time, much to Madame Camille's embarrassment. "The schools are no good here," she would remark. Pascal would have his dinner in his room, he never came out to dine with them. Madame Camille would take his plate to his room upstairs. He could hear her talking to him, urging him to keep his books away. "He is too shy to come in front of you," she apologized. "Normally, he eat dinner with his sisters, but not in front of guests."

It was a cold Sunday morning when Graham went out to the local church. It was an old building in Gothic style, perched high up on a hill. He had been there before but not during service. He didn't see Madame Camille there. "Maybe, she is busy cooking," he thought. The service was short, and he had time before lunch. He decided to take a stroll around. As he wandered to the backside of the church, he could see people with flowers kneeling over the tombstones. He walked past them, tipping his hat to some of the familiar faces in the village. He stopped at a tombstone and stared at it.

Someone called out his name. It was the local carpenter. He remembered he had an appointment with him. They walked down the hill towards his house.

It was Saturday, November the 22nd. Graham had a basket in his hand as he walked towards Madame Camille's cottage for his customary weekend visit. Florence opened the door and greeted him with a big smile. As he stepped inside, Madame Camille came out from the kitchen. She was in an apron and her hands were full of flour. "*Bonjour Monsieur*, I just finish the cake and will be with you shortly."

A few minutes later, she came in. "You know, it is Pascal's birthday today. He loves carrot cakes, I make one for him," she said. Graham got up and walked towards her. "I know, I brought some flowers for Pascal," he said, taking out the flowers from his basket and placing it in her hands.

Madame Camille looked at him and understood.

"Shall we walk to the church?" Graham suggested gently.

She nodded and they slowly made their way up the hill.

Piku & Chiki

I loved my garden. There was this big mango tree in the centre that seemed to touch the sky. At the far-left corner, was a guava tree that in its own right, was fairly tall, but dwarfed by its colossal neighbour. A hibiscus plant stood in one of the other corners – with its splendid display of pink flowers. Every day, my mother, would pluck them for her daily prayers but the next morning, it would be ready with a fresh supply. Then, there were the chrysanthemums and marigolds in the flower bed. The roses were carefully planted in colourful pots. Prakash, our gardener would shift these pots every day to ensure they get the right amount of sunlight. My job was to water these plants in the morning and evening – a task that I never got tired of. Occasionally I would get to dig up the soil around the plants, but Prakash would become restless very soon, as I would be more interested in the insects that came out from the loose soil. He would get me to clean the dry leaves and take on the task of loosening the soil himself.

We also had mischievous company in the garden – Piku and Chiki. Piku was the larger one, jumping from one branch to the other and sliding down the trunk of the immense mango tree. A dash across the garden and he would be up the guava tree in a jiffy, having miraculously picked up a nut on the way. His fur was deep grey, and his eyes shone with the curiosity of a new born baby. Chiki was his partner and more timid. She had light grey fur but big eyes. She would throw furtive glances all around before she dared come down the mango tree. I would sometimes see Piku waiting at the bottom of the tree, almost imploring Chiki to follow him to the guava tree. Once they were in the safety of the high trees, Chiki would lose her timidity and scutter along the branches with such energy that Piku would give up chasing her and wait for her to get tired and come to him. As dusk fell, the two would snuggle close to each other, nibbling each other's necks and falling asleep in quiet contentment.

Not everybody shared my enthusiasm for my garden though. My father watched me with disappointment as I walked barefoot in the garden, picking up a leaf or twig here and there. "This boy would come to no good, I warn you", he would yell at my mother. It would invariably lead to a lecture from him on how his colleague's son was making progress in studies and securing a bright future for himself. He had seen many of his siblings waste their life doing nothing and was always apprehensive that I would end that way. My sister sympathized with me but was too scared of our father to say anything. My mother, would try to protect me from the daily rebukes, skilfully avoiding it by reminding my father of some nonsensical task he was supposed to do at that time. As she spoke to my father, I could see her frantically waving her hand towards me, urging me to get back to my room through the back door. Over time I had learned to pick up these cues and devised some of my own as well. I would place a chair in the middle of the garden and pretend to be studying and would switch to reading loudly as I heard my father's footsteps approaching, ready to go to the local market. The moment he was out of the gate, the book would be flung on the ground and I would resume my activities in the garden.

After one of his many foreign trips, my father brought home a fancy digital camera. Soon, this became the most coveted possession of the house and was used in every possible situation. It recorded my mother's cooking, my sister's recitations and my brave attempts at singing. I would occasionally record my sister speaking in hushed tones with her friend and gleefully play it back in front of the full family. I recorded videos of the garden and its two important inhabitants – Piku and Chiki. The camera had a self-start and timer and I would set it up to start recording when their activities were at a peak. Back in my room after school, I would rewind the tape and watch the garden come to life.

One day, my father came home early from office and announced that he had bought tickets for all of us to go to Shimla, which was a famous hill station, a thousand miles away from where we lived. My sister and I jumped up with joy. My mother, as usual, started worrying about all the things that needed to get done at home exactly during the vacation. But eventually she came around and agreed that it was after all a good idea to go. The next few weeks flew by; I would count the days remaining for our trip. The last week was a flurry of activities – buying warm clothes, a new pair of shoes for me, a new dress for my sister and a shawl for my mother. Prakash would be reminded every day of his onerous task of tending to the garden in our absence. No amount of reassurance from his side seemed to satisfy my mother.

Finally, the day came when we boarded the train to Delhi that would connect us with the train to Shimla. Unknown to my father, I had devised my own way of staying in touch with garden. I had managed to place the camera close to the window of my bedroom that overlooked the garden and set up the daily timer to record the events of the garden on a regular basis. I only confided this arrangement to my sister – she was incredulous that I had dared to do all this without telling our father. Nonetheless, I was proud of myself, and felt like an adult during the entire trip to Shimla.

After two wonderful weeks, we came back home. Exhausted from the journey, I fell asleep as soon as my head hit the pillow. The sun was bright in the sky when I got out of bed. I sauntered into the garden, rubbing my eyes. The garden looked fresh as ever – Prakash had done a good job. A rustle in the mango tree and I looked up to see Chiki glancing at me. I waved at her and picked up a nut and tossed it towards her. But there was something wrong. She was not her playful self and wasn't scampering on the branches as she usually did. Piku was nowhere to be seen. I tried looking up the guava tree, but he wasn't there. I tried shaking the trees and throwing twigs up through the branches but to no avail. With a sinking heart, I realized that Piku had met with some misfortune. I felt sorry for Chiki but there was nothing I could do. The next few days, I kept a look out for Piku but was losing hope fast.

After a busy school week, the weekend arrived at last. As I lay in my room, fiddling with the camera, some commotion in the recording caught my attention. A flapping of wings and several squeals. I could now see a hawk in the screen holding something firmly in its talons. Zooming in, I could see it was Chiki. She was squealing and frantically trying to free herself from the clutches of the hawk. More squealing – and I saw Piku dashing through the branches. He was trying to get as close as possible to Chiki but feared the hawk. Meanwhile Chiki's body was growing limp with the pressure of the talons. In a final attempt to save his partner, Piku made a lunge at the hawk's feet and started biting at it. The next moment the hawk had Piku in its beak but in the scuffle Chiki slipped away. A flap of wings and the hawk was up in the sky with Piku in its beak.

I was dumbfounded. I must have sat there for a long time in stunned silence, before I heard my mother come in. She looked at me and immediately knew something was wrong. Between sobs, I recounted her the tragic incident. She held me close to her and rocked me gently. She must have said something to my father because that dinner I was spared from his lecture. My mother came to see me in bed. As I lay in my bed, I thought of Chiki and what she would be doing now without the soft comfort of Piku. I fell asleep as my mother stroked my hair through the night….

The Clock

Timothy hated Wednesdays. He would wake up complaining of some ailment or the other. But his mother would have none of this and would pack him off to school. He dreaded the afternoon as it drew closer. As he walked into the field, he could see the boys from the corner of his eyes, jeering at him. Avoiding their gaze and snide remarks, he would make his way to the starting line. At the sound of the whistle, the boys would sprint off for their weekly marathon. Timothy would join in gusto but within half a mile would fall behind. The remaining three miles would seem an eternity – jogging, walking and finally limping to the finish line, gasping for breath. His tormentors would be there waiting for him with a bucket of water. Drenched from head to toe, he would slump on the ground, his heart pounding and his chest heaving up and down, gulping down mouthfuls of air. As he walked back home, he would cheer up – glad that the ordeal was over.

But Timothy had a secret. A secret that no one in the world knew. Not even his twin brother Duncan. Every night, at bed time, he would take his secret out from the back of his cupboard. Unwrapping it from the scarf that concealed it, he would place it on his desk, supported against his pile of books. His excitement would rise as he looked at its curly hands and the patterned face. It looked like an ordinary clock except that it had a counter for the year. Every night he would set the clock to a different year and get transported back to history.

He had seen Tutankhamen's reign, the battle of Hastings, the exploits of Genghiz Khan and the grandeur of the Mughal kings in India. He witnessed the plots of deception and treason hatched in the palaces, the opulence of the kings that contrasted with the penury of their subjects. History was his favourite subject in school, and he would have a hard time sticking to facts in the text book than what he had seen the previous night. It was only this morning that in response to a question in the class, his History teacher had remarked, "Now Timothy, where on earth have you read that? We all know that Alexander the Great was a successful general, leading his army to epic victories. Why are you saying that it was actually his half-brother who devised the plans for the battles?"

The next lecture was on Maths. A new teacher had arrived in school who was more interested in teaching the history behind Maths, than algebraic equations. He turned his back to the class, picked up a dusty chalk and proceeded to write the number zero on the board. The next thirty minutes were spent in a lecture of the importance of zero in our lives and how our forefathers had discovered the power of this unique number a thousand years ago.

That night, after dinner, as he turned the counters of the clock, the Maths lecture must have been playing in mind when he set the clock to year zero.

He was cold. There was snow everywhere. The wind was howling. "It must be the Ice Age," Timothy thought. There were no signs of any life, even the trees seemed to be straining under the weight of the snow. Thump! Thump! Thump! He whirled around to see an elephant like creature running across the plains. "It is a woolly mammoth," he exclaimed. Soon he could hear shouts and an army of people with spears emerged, chasing the mammoth. He joined the group but found it hard to keep pace with them as their muscular bodies sprinted through the vast white plains. After half an hour, the chase was abandoned, and he could see the men huddled around each other making gestures and patting each other on the back. He stepped closer to have a good look at them. They had big foreheads, muscular bodies with wide chests but shorter than most of the people he knew. "I have seen them somewhere before," he thought. "Was it in the book I read the other week or in the movie I saw last month. It was in the Natural History Museum," he said, his memory came back. "Neanderthal Man!" he exclaimed. They seemed to recognize him, hugging and slapping him on his back with such force, that he almost fell.

They made their way through the hills. The path led to some caves and they stopped at a rather large one. Somebody shouted out from the group and soon a shrivelled face peered from the cave. A smile of recognition followed by a wave and out came a dozen people. Stepping closer, he realized that they were women with large bracelets around their necks, arms and legs. Seeing the men, they stepped into some kind a dance, stamping their ground with their feet and raising their hands high up in the air. Finally, they all trooped inside, Timothy following them. Someone was arranging branches in the middle and another grinding some kind of stone. A spark lit in the night and the branches caught fire. This was greeted by a rapturous shout from the group. Large stone slabs lay on the ground with twigs and leaves on them. "These must be their beds," Timothy thought.

A large stone shaped in the form of a bowl lay in the centre. There were three women who were using sticks to stir its contents. He leaned over and almost threw up. It was blood.

He made his way to the back of the cave and was surprised to find another chamber there. There were more people here. But they seemed thinner and weaker. Once in a while somebody would shriek out in pain as his wound would be tended to. He could see a man with a leg that was so twisted that it seemed to curl behind his body. His mouth was tied with some kind of a belt to prevent him from screaming in pain.

Timothy quickly crossed over – unable to bear this sight any longer. A dark passage led him deep into the cave. The din of voices was growing louder. He tripped over something hard and fell flat on his face. Turning over, he found a dozen young faces staring at him. They were saying something in a strange language and miraculously he could understand them. "Who are you? Why are you here? Have you lost your way?" A few of them helped him get up on his feet. They were touching his face, pulling at his shirt, running their fingers over the buttons and smelling his hair. They were most amused with his glasses – he taught them how to wear it and they looked funny in their feathery dresses with his glasses on. He talked about how he lived, his brother, his school and his friends. They listened intently but didn't seem to understand. Once in a while somebody would clap his hands and they would roll over each other in the ground, laughing.

Their laughter was interrupted by the most deafening roar Timothy had ever heard. The next moment he heard shouts from the other side of cave. There was some commotion going on. He could hear the rush of footsteps and people shouting at each other. The men he had met earlier, now emerged in the cave chamber he was in. Some were carrying the wounded on their shoulders. "Run! Run!", they urged the youngsters. Someone in the crowd grabbed Timothy's hand and they ran outside in the cold. They must have run only a short distance before his legs started giving way. The same burning sensation and cramps. He was exhausted and slumped on to the hard ice. One of the young men helped him to his feet. Timothy was gasping for breath. "I can't run any longer," he said. The youngster took something off his waist and placed it in his hands. "Tie this around yourself, this will give you strength," he said. It was a belt with beads of ivory stuck on its side. "Now, let's go. The lions are closing in," he urged.

As they started again, Timothy felt a sudden surge of energy pervading through his body. Faster and faster, they sprinted through the dark plains and caught up with the rest of the group. As they neared the edge of the plains, they could see the shadowy figures of the pine trees. Timothy's feet slipped and he hurtled down a deep crevice, flailing his arms around...

He woke up with a start. It was a bright Wednesday morning. As his mother saw him off to the school bus stand, she asked him if he had packed everything for the day, surprised to see him so calm that day. He nodded and got in the bus, waving to his mother as he found a seat by the window. Later that afternoon, at the whistle, Timothy was still thinking about last night, when somebody pushed him across the line. He started running. Five hundred yards, one mile, two miles, he kept going. Very soon he caught up with the other boys and waving to them crossed the finish line in a breeze.

His tormentors arrived a few minutes later. They stared at him in disbelief, some started pulling out his shoes to see if he had any special boots on. One of them jeered, "Are you indeed Timothy? Or is it Duncan today?"

Timothy smiled and patted the ivory belt under his shirt. He now had a new secret.

Bravery

"Can someone call Ravi please," called Sharda from the kitchen. Her two children – Rahul and Neha were already at the table, banging on the plates and relishing the aroma of hot food drifting from the kitchen. Their dad, Mahesh, had just returned from office and emerged out of the washroom folding the sleeves of his *kurta*. He settled himself at the head of the table and called out to Sharda, "I am starving – can you bring the food please?" He wasn't in a good mood and the children knew why. They knew it was best not to provoke him, so they fell silent.

"Someone, please go and get Ravi," said Sharda as she came out of the kitchen. Neha got up to get her brother down from his room.

"As it is, we have no end to our troubles," Mahesh was saying. "I have met the doctors today and they don't have good news for us. We cannot find a match with any of the donors and even if there is one, there are at least a hundred patients ahead of Neha. I have no idea when we will get a donor and date for the operation. As for Ravi, he is in his own world, creating his own worries out of thin air while we are faced with such big decisions in our life."

Meanwhile, Neha had found Ravi in his room craning his neck out of his window. "Ravi, now come on... nothing has fallen down. Don't worry about anything - everybody is waiting for you downstairs," she said gently. Ravi looked over his shoulder and she could see the anxiety in his eyes. It was all too familiar to her, but she knew how to handle it. Gently she took Ravi's hand and pulled him away from the window. As she led him down the stairs, she kept re-assuring him that things will be alright, and he should cheer up.

"Here comes my brave son," exclaimed Mahesh. "What were you worrying about now?"

Sharda quickly tried to change the topic and got busy serving food to the family. She knew too well how these conversations could end. It was only last week that Mahesh had got so angry that he had thrown his food at Ravi.

The lentils were good, and it must have calmed Mahesh's nerves. "I will speak to Dr Kohli," he said. "He has the right connections in the hospital. I am sure he will help find us a good kidney donor for Neha and help push her up the queue. My father taught him Chemistry at school and he still respects our family a lot. I am hopeful he will do something about it."

"Don't worry so much," said Sharda. "We need to be patient and have faith in God." She was putting up a brave face but was worried about things inside.

As she lay on her bed, her mind was in turmoil. It had not been easy with Ravi the last few years. His worries had increased a lot. Sometimes he would get stuck in the corridor thinking that he had dropped something and not being able to find it. At other times, he would imagine that he had unknowingly hurt somebody walking by their house and that the police could come in any moment. Doctors hadn't been of much help and he was undergoing a new therapy on a trial basis. His school, however, had been very supportive and she was glad that at least his teachers understood his problems. Back at home, Rahul wasn't very helpful and had no time for Ravi. He was three years older than him and preferred to keep to his own. But Neha, who was a year younger than Ravi, loved him a lot. Sharda smiled as she thought of how Neha and Ravi would spend hours together in their room, gossiping away. And now, with Neha's diagnosis, it couldn't have come at a worse time...

"Mummy, I am scared." Her thoughts were interrupted by Neha who had come into the room. "Now, don't start crying again Neha," said Sharda. "Everything will be alright. Don't worry about what Papa is saying, he is just a little hassled with all the hospital visits. Dr Kohli will help us. In a few months' time, you will have a new kidney and we will go to Machu Picchu in the holidays. Papa has already booked tickets for all of us." Neha's face brightened up at the thought of going to Peru. "Ravi will enjoy a lot in the mountains, he loves to walk in the hills," Neha said. Sharda was glad that Neha had cheered up and took her hand and clasped it in her own.

The next day, Mahesh came back late in the evening. He seemed tired and distraught. Sharda came to him as he sank into the sofa. "What is the matter, dear? Did you meet Dr Kohli? What did he say?" She looked at Mahesh anxiously.

"I can't believe it," Mahesh said. "It is such a bureaucratic process. He said he can't help us – we must wait for our turn. Even after that, it is such a gamble. Sometimes the operations are not successful, and the body rejects the donor's organ. Neha's blood group is so unique, we will be extremely lucky to find a donor."

Sharda realized that Ravi and Neha were in the room listening to their conversation, so she quickly escorted them out of the room. "It is better they don't get to hear all these details," she thought.

The next day, at the dinner table, the mood was sombre. Even Sharda, who always managed to put up a smiling face, seemed subdued. Rahul was busy munching away at the chicken. Ravi was eating quietly, and Neha was fidgeting with her food. Mahesh had a mouthful of naan when Ravi blurted out, "We did a blood test in our school lab today."

Mahesh stopped eating and glared at Ravi. "That's great but we are not interested in your blood test. By the way, when did you return home? Did you finish the homework on time today?" Mahesh was clearly not in a

35

good mood. Sharda looked anxiously around the table and tried to make some small talk to defuse the situation.

"My blood group is the same as Neha's," Ravi continued. "I also read in the internet about good donors."

Mahesh was now getting angry and the colour was rising in his cheek. "Of course, your blood group will be the same as Neha's. After all you are her brother," he said sarcastically. "Now you had better shut up and finish your food."

"I want to give my kidney to Neha," said Ravi softly.

Mahesh almost choked on his food. Sharda's hand went to her mouth in disbelief. Rahul and Neha stared at Ravi. Ravi was looking down at his plate and muttering softly, "I only need one kidney and Neha needs one. We are of the same family; her body will not reject it."

Sharda could see Mahesh struggling to contain his tears. She got up and went to Ravi and hugged him and burst out crying. They went upstairs together, Neha and Rahul followed them.

Later that night, as Neha and Ravi lay on the bed, Neha whispered ' Aren't you scared Ravi?"

"I am," said Ravi. "But I want to be brave like you. If you have something of me inside you, I will always feel that we are together, and I will be strong. My worries will not trouble me anymore."

Neha hugged her brother tightly...and they fell asleep talking about the mountains of Machu Picchu.

Dolphins

The waves were up to his neck, but the strong hands of Tom steadied his legs on the sea floor. As the water receded, it left behind a treasure of shells. He stooped to pick up a bright orange one, gingerly holding it between his tiny fingers.

"Let's go home Jack, called out Lisa from the beach. Soon, he was being dragged along the beach, his wobbly feet unsteady in the wet sand. Wrapping a towel around his slender body, they made their way back to their home.

It was a daily ritual. Buckets and spades in tow, Jack would head to the beach at noon with his Mum, Lisa. His father, Tom, would join them during the weekends. Seaweeds, shells, pebbles – all were fascinating for Jack. By the end of the day, he would have a treasure trove of shells to take back home. He would be allowed to take home only a few though. Once at home, Jack would be at the window watching the children play among the waves.

Sometimes, if the weather was good during the weekend, they would venture out further in the sea in their red boat. Jack would have to wear a life vest and would be clearly displeased with this contraption. Constantly tugging at the strings, he would try to wriggle out of it. The call of the sea gulls would distract him, and he would try to lunge at them as they dived into the water. Lisa would keep a watchful eye as Tom steered the boat deeper into the sea. The big ships could be seen faintly at a distance. They seemed motionless in the turbulent waters. Sometimes they would see shoals of fish near the surface – a sign that the larger fish were not far away. And sure enough, the tuna and dolphins would be seen tearing through the shoals as they hunted their favourite prey. If the sea was calm, Tom would jump into the water and lift Jack off the boat into the cold water. Jack would squeal with delight as the fish touched his bare legs. He would try to grab them by his hands, but they would easily give him a slip. It was different with the dolphins. They would encircle the boat, splashing their tails and raising their snouts out of the water as they passed close to Jack. He had got used to them by now, brushing against their silken bodies. As they jostled against each other in the waters, Jack would be thrown around and Tom would have to reach out and grab him, lest he drifts too far away from the boat. The dolphins would follow the boat around, frolicking in the water and raising their snouts as Jack strained to touch them from the boat.

It was a bright Friday afternoon, when Lisa received a call on the beach. Hanging up, she called out to Jack, who had a disappeared into a hole he had dug himself. "We must go home Jack," said Lisa, collecting the bucket and spades as she waited for Jack to emerge. Jack wasn't amused and let his displeasure know by lying down flat on the beach. But Lisa had to go, so she picked him up and slung him over her shoulder. They made their way to their cottage, Jack's tiny feet beating against Lisa's arm.

Lisa settled Jack in his bed. She had to go to the hospital to see her friend and Jack would be safer asleep at home. She would return in an hour, much before Jack woke up. Picking up her sunglasses, she went out carefully locking the door behind her. As she got into the car, her thoughts turned to her friend. Katie had sounded scared during the call and she had offered to go to the hospital with her to see the doctor. At the hospital, Katie livened up on seeing her and hugged her. Two hours later, she was back on the road home. The weather had turned during her absence. It had become windy and overcast. As she came into the driveway, she remembered the bucket and spades that she had left near the back door. I must have put them in the shed, she thought as she made her way into the back garden. Picking up the bucket, her heart froze. The door was ajar. Frantically, she ran upstairs to Jack's room. He wasn't in his bed. Her heart racing, she opened the door of her bedroom, but no Jack. She called out to him...but was only greeted with silence. She felt dizzy as she rushed down the stairs and ran towards the beach. It was getting dark and people had packed up and were making their way home. As she reached the edge of the water, her eyes scanned the expanse of the beach but there was no sign of Jack. She was going crazy with fear. She suddenly remembered their boat. Maybe he had gone there, she thought, as she ran towards the docks. Gasping for breath, she reached the docks, only to find that their boat had disappeared. They had to buy a new rope to tie the boat to the pier, it then occurred to her. But the water was so calm here that the boat hardly moved from its position even if left untied. But not today. She sank into the ground with her hands covering her face. Something hard pricked her feet as she tried to get up. It was the bright orange shell. "Jack must be in the boat," she agonized. Her hands shook as she spoke with Tom. His voice calmed her a bit. "Don't panic," he said. "I am nearly there and will be at the pier in a few moments." She stood there waiting for Tom, gazing at the sea as darkness enveloped the shores.

It was 7 p.m. when the coast guard got the call. Realizing that the sea was rough, they scrambled into a helicopter. As they searched through the night, they picked up the red boat, bobbing up on the sea. A diver lowered himself on top of the boat as the helicopter hovered above. He could see a figure slumped on the boat as he got close. It was Jack. Breathing a sigh of relief, he reached out for Jack and pulled him by his shirt. Jack had fainted from exhaustion, but he was lucky to be alive.

As the pair were pulled into the helicopter, the diver peered over to where the boat was. The boat had disappeared. "That is odd. It was here a minute ago. It must have sunk," he thought, as his eyes scanned the waters for signs of the boat.

All he could see were bubbles and the faint silhouettes of the dolphins, swimming in the cold waters.

The Letter

It had been a long flight. The snow hadn't helped as well. Luckily, the flight took off, only three hours behind schedule. I could feel the heavy air as I stepped outside the airport, into the chaotic roads of Delhi. Dodging the cars weaving through the airport parking bays, I made my way to the grey Toyota. Rumali took my suitcase and put it next to him in the passenger seat. I got into the car, greeted by the familiar whiff of lavender. "How's everything Rumali?" I asked, as I tried to get the data connection on my phone. "Everything is alright.... but Madam ..." his voice trailed off. I nodded and decided to change the topic. "We'll go to Jaipur tomorrow. Can you come at 9 a.m. sharp?" I asked him. "Sure Sir, I will be there." Thirty minutes later, we were at home. Rumali placed my suitcase on the veranda, thanked me for the money and handed over the keys to the house.

It was a strange feeling, opening the lock of the house and stepping into the vacuum inside. I remembered the last time I had come home. That was two years ago. my mother was at the gate when Rumali blew the horn. She had seemed frail and weak. As I took her hands, I could see the folds of the soft skin over her wrist. "You must take care of yourself," I had told her as we walked inside.

The dining table seemed bigger than usual this time. "Maybe because it doesn't have the piles of fruits and flowers that mother kept on it – her daily offering to the myriad Gods and Goddesses," I thought. I crossed over to the adjoining room, my bedroom of childhood. The bed was still strong but hadn't been slept in for decades. I placed the suitcase in a corner and went to freshen up.

I must have fallen asleep, for it was dark when I woke up. I found my way to the switch board and turned on the tube light. I blinked as the lamp came on. The photo frames stared at me from the mantelpiece. My father had died five years ago; mom had learnt to live alone without him, learning to do things she had never done in her life. But now that she was gone…. everything in the house seemed to be stuck in time.

"I need to open her trunk," I thought. "I must remove the valuables from the house – it is not safe to keep them here any longer." I stepped into her bedroom. The dressing table stood next to the door with used *Bindis* stuck to the mirror. A Cuticura powder lay upturned on a plastic tray, next to the tub of Nivea cream. I opened the Nivea; there was still a lot left of it. Removing the strands of hair stuck to the box, I placed it carefully back on the plastic tray. The music system was on the table, with its gaping hole, which was once a CD changer. I looked underneath the bed and pulled out the trunk. My mother never locked the trunk. Shawls, sweaters, bed sheets, everything was neatly folded. My fingers felt something metallic. I pulled them out – they were the Army gallantry medals of my brother, Sujoy.

"Mom loves you more than me," Sujoy would complain. "You get the best piece of fish, an extra spoon of rice pudding and get to sit in the best spot at the dining table, right across the TV." Mother would try to pacify Sujoy, giving him an extra sweet that day. But it was true that I was the more pampered child. She would always take my side. Once Sujoy and I had a fight and I got a nasty cut near my left eye, hitting the corner of a chair while chasing him. I was so angry with Sujoy at that time that I blamed the cut on him. That night Sujoy got a thrashing from our father.

But I loved Sujoy, he was my best friend. He was stronger than me and saved me from the bullies in school. I remembered a fight when he had broken the front teeth of one such bully. We would spend hours going around the city in our bicycles. Sujoy was the more daring of us and he would ride it on one wheel with his arms high up in the air. How I admired his skills!

Then came the war and every household was supposed to send one member to fight at the front. I remember the night when the local councillor came to our house. Our parents sent us to our rooms and argued with him for hours. I could hear my father shouting and my mother crying. It was ten in the night when the councillor left. Mom came in, red-faced and went straight to the kitchen. Our father was pacing in his room. She gave us dinner and asked us to have it in our rooms. They did not eat that night. The next day, our father called both of us in his room. Mom was there as well, trying not to look at us. Our father was trying to be calm, but his expressions betrayed his feelings. He tried to say a few things that made no sense. Finally, he announced that the councillor had not agreed to their pleas of exempting Sujoy and me from the war duty and they had decided that Sujoy would go to the war front. "He is the more adventurous and stronger of you two. After all, it is only going be a year before he will be back," our father reasoned. Mom burst out crying and went away from the room. Later, she came to Sujoy's room and talked with him throughout the night. I was glad that Mom loved Sujoy as much as she loved me.

A month later, Sujoy left for the war. He would write to us every week and talk about how many friends he had made and how he had started to love the food in the canteen. Months passed by and we started planning for his return. In those days, Mom would dote on me even more. She would sit in my room for hours, looking out of the window, as I pored over my books. One morning, my father went out for his morning walk, when someone told him about an attack on the army camp the previous night. He rushed back home but fainted on the way. A friend of his saw him fall and informed us. Mom and I rushed to his side. Luckily, he wasn't hurt much. I ran to get the newspaper from the local shop as my father switched on the TV. There was indeed a blast and several casualties. It was late in the evening when the call came from the army camp. Our father took the call; Sujoy was no more.

My father never recovered from the shock; he died a year later. Mom tended for him during these days, keeping herself busy. Rumali would come every day in the evening to take Mom to the local temple. She would spend her evenings there and come back home before dinner. We did not talk about Sujoy at home, we dealt with his loss in our own way, individually. I became a recluse; my books were my only companions. When I got a scholarship to study abroad, I decided to go. "I will be there for a few years only, and then come back home," I told Mom. She did not say anything but packed my things and gave me supplies of home-made sweets and *namkeens*. It has been fifteen years since then, and my visits had become less and less frequent over the years. Mom passed away a year ago and I had come now to wind up her affairs at the bank and at the local council.

As I kept the medals aside, my eyes fell on a white envelope. It had no address; I was curious and opened it to find a photograph and a letter. I stared at the photograph – there was a couple holding a child in their arms. I had no idea who they were. I opened the letter.

"Dear Manik, I will not be there when you read this letter. I want to let you know a truth that I kept from you. The photograph in this envelope is that of your parents. They were very close friends of ours. You were very small when we went to Chandigarh by car. We met with a big accident on the way and lost your parents. We wanted to be good parents for you, and I hope we have been able to. I hope you will understand and forgive us for keeping this truth from you. I love you with all my heart. May all your wishes come true. Yours…. Mother.

I was curled up in the bed when Rumali came next morning. "Jaipur, Sir?" he asked, as I settled in the back seat of the Toyota, avoiding his gaze.

I shook my head. "Take me to the temple," I said, my voice choking.

Rumali began to say something but I stopped him with a wave of my hand as he looked at me through the overhead mirror.

One more word...and my heart would burst.

For Humanity's Sake

It was a large room. A painting hung at the far end of the room. I couldn't make out what it was from this distance. A huge table filled the room. At the far end of this table, a group of people were discussing something animatedly. As I went closer, I could make out some faces – two familiar faces and the rest unknown. My friend Anand was there, writing vigorously on what seemed to be a large pile of papers. Ajay was leaning on the table – intently talking to the lady opposite him. The other members were listening eagerly.

"It is a case of natural selection gentlemen," Ajay was saying. "Only folks with the best intellect and physical strength will survive the millennia. We must move ahead and hopefully the less able will either catch-up or get exterminated. Darwin's theory is simple, and we need to accept that."

"That is precisely the issue," said the lady. "Higher intellect comes at a cost. The cost is instability of the mind and the lack of balance. Imagine if we had a billion Einstein's in this world today – do we think the world would be a better place to live in or more chaotic? Einstein could not find the way to his hotel and couldn't easily accept ideas that challenged his theories. How can the world be collaborative and achieve peaceful coexistence?"

"There is a cost to everything we do," shot back Ajay. "The benefits outweigh the costs and that is all that is important. Smart people will ensure continued dominance of the human race and everybody will enjoy the progress as we go along. In any case, we can't stop the process of evolution, so we better accept it and move on."

"We need be aware of threats to our existence," said the man with horn-rimmed glasses. "The omnipresent germs and microbes are in the same process of evolution as we are. As we try to secure our lives with better antibiotics, these microbes are constantly mutating to beat our defences. We have to slow down their evolutionary process even as we speed up ours."

The gentleman next to the lady was busy brushing off specks from his suit but sat up suddenly. "We need to think a million years from now and ask the question – Will humans continue to rule this earth? I think the answer is 'NO' and the reason, bizarre as it may sound, is our own smartness. Not because we will develop weapons of mass extinction or get wiped out by deadly microbes but because our ever-evolving brains cannot remain stable. This instability will be our nemesis, when remembering or doing simple things may well become impossible. We need to slow down the process of evolution of our brains."

"So, what is the plan?" Anand had stopped writing and was staring at the group. "You are the experts and we need a plan to avoid this looming catastrophe."

"I have an idea," I exclaimed. The faces turned towards me.

"Why don't we create a selection of people, who will live a secluded life – cut off from the rest of the world. They will have access to the 'normal' world for certain things but will be broadly excluded from the advancements being made. The process of evolution is hastened by our own advancements that exercise our brain further, making it sharper. By stopping this access to stimulants, we will achieve a rate of development of the brain that is so infinitesimally small, that it will not reach any level of instability before the next meteorite strikes the earth."

"This is complicated. Why don't we just do a plain and simple geographical or economic divide," cried Ajay. "We can use the next UN meeting to table this motion."

"It is not as simple as you think Ajay," I responded. "Genetics is the basis of all evolution and genetic codes do not always follow geographical divides. Besides, we have to create pure groups of people who have a natural propensity to evolve at a slower rate. Any contamination of this group will defeat the purpose. You may have to divide families as part of this process."

"Fair enough," sighed Ajay, resignedly.

The AI expert in the room was getting visibly excited, rubbing his hands gleefully. "My algorithms will identify these people very precisely. I will need to access the gene data pool, but that should be easy. We have done this before."

My thoughts, meanwhile, had turned to my family: Will we get split? What if one of us doesn't make it to the same group? What does exclusion mean? What happens to my house and the new TV that I bought? We have booked a trip to Mauritius – will we be allowed to go there? My mind was in turmoil…endless questions were welling up.

The music was getting louder. '*Pal Pal Dil Ke Paas, Tum Rahti Ho…* '.

"Why are we playing this number, I need some peace," I thought.

A nudge on my back and I see Madhu. "Tea is ready."

I dragged myself out of bed. Glad that it was just a dream. Or was it?

White Lilies

Sixty, fifty-nine, fifty-eight……..four, three. A rumbling of tyres and the bus came in sight. It braked with a jolt, raising a cloud of dust all around. I covered my face with my hands and peered through them at the door. One by one the boys and girls jumped out of the bus, glad that the day was over. I waved as Lucy emerged. She looked at me and her face lit up in a smile. As she came towards me, I held out my hand for her bag. She used to protest earlier but not anymore. I swung the bag over my shoulder, feeling the weight of the books. She slipped her hand in mine and we walked down the road, Lucy chattering away all the way.

It had been a long day for her, and many things had happened at school. Somebody had pulled her hair during the morning assembly, the teacher's chair was hidden in a corner in the Maths class, two of her best friends had kept a secret from her and therefore no longer qualified to be her best friends. I would ask a question here and there but mostly listened. From time to time, she would ask me a question to make sure I was paying attention. For me, listening to her voice was enough, it filled my heart with joy. But over time I had learned to respond at the appropriate moments. At the end of the road, we would have to part ways and would stand there gossiping, as hordes of school children brushed past us. Finally, the road would become deserted and we would turn towards our houses.

The memories of school were still fresh in my mind. They weren't nice. I struggled at almost everything that was taught there. The Maths class was a nightmare for me. I would try to hide behind my desk, trying to disappear from the piercing gaze of the teacher. But she would invariably pick up on me, making me an example for the class. The only thing I looked forward to was the Art class. Here, I could let my mind roam free and paint in the colours I liked. Despite my efforts, I hardly got any encouragement from the teacher. "All this is fine," he would say. "But you need to be good at Maths to do anything in life."

It was in the Art class that I met Lucy. She studied in the same form but in a different section. Sometimes Art classes would be conducted jointly with other groups and during one of those occasions, I found myself sitting next to her. I had finished sketching the forest when I looked at her sheet. She hadn't even started. She looked at me and smiled and said softly "I have no idea what to do, can you help me please?" This was a first time that anybody in the school had asked me for help. We quickly exchanged our sheets and I furiously worked on her sheet, just in time to submit to the teacher. The teacher looked at her sheet and then at her, surprised to see so much progress. I put a finger to my lips, as she looked at me nervously. The teacher let her go and I heaved a sigh of relief.

I saw her again in the evening bus and she waited for me as I got down at the bus stand. I smiled and started walking with her. She had moved in to the school recently. Her father was in the Army, a transferable job and this was supposed to be his last transfer. Her mother was a housewife but had more engagements that her father. She had a younger brother, who was not old enough to go to school. She stopped and looked at me. "You are not telling me anything about yourself," she said. I stammered a few facts about myself, that my father was an accountant and my mother worked in the local library. I was the only child of my parents and had been in the school since...I stopped, and she looked at me. I tried to hide my tears and looked away. She put her hand on my shoulder. "Don't worry about school, I find it hard too. You are so good at painting, I wish I could be like you," she said gently. "Now let's talk about something else." As we parted ways at the end of the road, I walked towards my home, happy and proud of myself after a long time.

Meanwhile, my parents were getting increasingly worried about my performance at school. I could hear them in their room talking about me late into the night. My ordeal at school continued unbated, I was struggling to cope with the pressure. The only thing I looked forward to was the journey back home. I would rush out of the class room at the sound of the closing bell. My eyes strained for Lucy as she made her way to the bus. We would sit next to each other and she would talk about the day's events in the school. I would listen to her and wonder how much she enjoyed school.

Lucy was a sincere student and during exams, she would take out her notes and study on the way home. I was just happy to be with her and would hold her bag in my lap as she prepared for her exams. Sometimes, she would try to explain topics to me. I didn't want to disappoint her, so pretended to understand her and distracted her attention whenever she wanted to ask me a question about it. Her mother baked well, and she would get cakes and cookies for school. She would save some for me and would dig them out from her bag in the bus. I liked the coffee and walnut cakes a lot and she would ask her mother for a large portion on those days.

On Fridays, Lucy was allowed to return home late. We would head over to the lake, which was a short walk from the bus stand. Summer was the season of lilies and a carpet of white lilies adorned the periphery of the lake. We would sit there feeding the ducks with the crumbs of cake from her box. She told me about the places she had visited with her father. She had even been in a fighter jet - it was a scary experience. I squeezed her hand, glad that she was there with me now.

The exams had been over a week, when my parents received a call from the headmaster. I saw them go out with tensed expressions. I was in my room when they returned home. My father came to see me. "Your mother is not feeling well, she is taking rest in her room," he said. He sat beside me and explained what the Headmaster had said. I was a child with special needs and this school was not right for me. I will need to go to a special school for a few hours every morning. It was in the neighbouring town. "But don't worry," he said. "Our driver will drop you and pick you up every day."

That night, I lay awake in bed. It was a relief not to go to school but Lucy...I fell asleep exhausted.

The next day, I stayed at home. In the evening, I made my way to the bus stop. As Lucy got down, she spotted me and ran towards me. "Where were you? Why didn't you come to school? I have some cookies in my bag." She looked at my face and stopped. We walked slowly home, her hand in mine. For once, she was silent. We didn't speak as we parted ways at the corner. I walked home, with a heavy heart.

It had now become a routine. I would be back from my school in the afternoon and would wait eagerly for the clock to turn five. I would head out towards the bus stand and count the last sixty seconds to when the bus would arrive.

Years passed by and Lucy was now in the university in Nice. She would write to me from there and I would read her letters every night. She had been to the Alps with her friends. It was beautiful; She had bought a cap for me from the local market there. She had learnt to play the piano. And yes, she was good at it. Good that they didn't have any painting classes at the university. Her professors were not as nice as her school teachers. They would take a lecture and then sit for hours in their offices, doing nothing.

I waited for her vacations, when she would be home. We would go to the lake or for a walk in nearby forests. It was a cloudy evening during her summer break, when she said to me softly, "You know, I am getting married. I met him at the annual ball in my university. He works in the Royal Air Force and lives in Edinburgh." I looked at her and nodded in understanding. She took my hand and said, "But I will write to you. You need to write as well so that I know that you are well and taking care of yourself." I nodded in silence, too overwhelmed to say anything.

A month later she got married. I went to see her off at the station. From a distance, I could see her hugging her parents and her brother, who had now grown into a tall boy. She looked at me over her brother's shoulders. Our eyes met and she quickly turned away to pick up her suitcase. I raised my hand to wave at her but held it back half way through. I went over to the lake that day, unable to stop the hot tears rolling down my cheeks. The lilies were beginning to wither away, their petals strewn on the waters of the lake.

A year passed by and Lucy had not written to me. I had started to teach children painting at a nearby school. I loved being with them, helping them give expressions to their ideas and feelings. Back at home, I would be all by myself in my room, looking out for the postman. But it would only be letters from the school or parents of my students. I tried to keep myself happy, reading Lucy's letters from the university over and over again.

One day, our neighbours Mr and Mrs Johnson came home for dinner. They sat in the living room talking about how people's lives had changed so much in our town. I caught Mrs Johnson telling my mother. "Nowadays, marriage is such a gamble. You know Major Smith's daughter, Lucy?" "Oh yes," replied my mother. "Didn't she get married last year?" "Yes," said Mrs Johnson in a hushed tone, "but she is back now. It didn't work out with the boy. She suffered in silence for a year but couldn't take it anymore and came back to her parents yesterday." The conversation went on. But my heart was racing. It was six in the evening; sunset was still an hour away. I stepped out on the street and started walking.

I found her by the lake. She did not look up as I slid next to her.

The ducks were at a distance, wading in the still waters of the lake. The lilies had gone, it would be a year before they bloomed again. We sat there silently watching the sun set, her head resting on my shoulders.

Printed in Great Britain
by Amazon